For William and Timothy
~ J.S.
For Nina, with love
~ T.W.

This edition produced 2008 for
BOOKS ARE FUN LTD
1680 Hwy 1 North, Fairfield, Iowa, IA 52556

by LITTLE TIGER PRESS
An imprint of Magi Publications
1 The Coda Centre, 189 Munster Road, London SW6 6AW
www.littletigerpress.com

Originally published in Great Britain 1996
by Little Tiger Press, London

Printed in China
ISBN 978-1-84506-915-5

1 2 3 4 5 6 7 8 9 10

Shhh!

by Julie Sykes

illustrated by Tim Warnes

It was Christmas Eve,

and Santa was in a jolly mood.

"Jingle bells,

jingle bells,

jingle all the way!" sang Santa noisily,

as he loaded all the toys onto the sleigh.

"SHHH, SANTA," whispered the reindeer.

"You have to be quiet tonight.

You mustn't wake the children!"

"I'll try not to," said Santa. "But I *do* like singing!"

NORTH
POLE

Over the moonlit world they sped,
toward the sleeping children.

Santa was so excited that he forgot
to land on the roof of the first house.

"BUSY,
 BUSY,
 BUSY BEE!" roared Santa, coming down
to land in the yard, and meeting a friendly cat.
"Happy Christmas, Cat!"
The cat waved her tail in the air.
"SHHH, SANTA," she whispered back.
"You mustn't wake the children!"
     "Of course I won't," said Santa,
          jumping out of the sleigh.

All the house was sleeping
as Santa threw the sack over his
shoulder and tiptoed along the
path toward the back door.
Only the snowman was awake.

"OOH,
 OOH,
 OOH-OOPS!" cried Santa,
slide on a patch of ice and crashing
to the ground.

"SHHH, SANTA," whispered the snowman.
"You mustn't wake the children!"
"Sorry," said Santa, picking himself up
and bouncing indoors. "But Christmas *is*
my favorite time of year!"

When he reached the Christmas tree,
Santa stopped bouncing, and pulled
some presents from his sack.

A jack-in-the-box burst out,
and made Santa jump in surprise.

"HEE, HEE,
 HEE, HEE,
 HEE, HEE, HEE!"
laughed Santa,
clapping his hands.
"SHHH, SANTA," whispered
the family's dog, who was
watching the fun.
"You mustn't wake the children!"

"Mustn't wake the children," agreed Santa. He put his finger to his lips, and crept across the room . . .

. . . but he didn't notice the
tinsel, trailing all over the floor –
until it was too late.
"BUMPITY,
  BUMPITY,
  BUMP!" boomed Santa,
landing on a roller skate.
He skidded across the carpet,
and fell headfirst into the fireplace.
It was a good thing the fire was out!

"AAH,
 AAH,
 AAH-CHOO!" sneezed Santa,
rubbing the soot from his nose.
"SHHH, SANTA," said the kitten
sleepily from an armchair by the hearth.
"You mustn't wake the children!"
        "Yes, we must be quiet," whispered Santa,
        scrambling to his feet.

Santa picked up his sack and hurried back to his sleigh. There were lots more visits to make before Christmas Day, but at last his sack was empty.

Santa rubbed his eyes sleepily and called,
"Home, Reindeer!"
And with a toss of their heads and a jingle of bells,
the reindeer leapt into the sky.

"HO, HO, HO!" shouted Santa loudly.

"Here we are, home at last!"

"SHHH, SANTA," he added quietly to himself.

"I know, I mustn't wake the children!"

It had been a busy night, and Santa
felt very tired.
He made himself a cup of hot cocoa,
put on his slippers, lay back in his armchair
and fell fast asleep . . .

". . . z z z z z,"
snored Santa.
"MUNCH,
MUNCH,
CRUNCH!"
went the reindeer,
as they tucked into
their supper.
"SHHH!" squeaked
Santa's little mouse.

"YOU MUSTN'T WAKE SANTA!"